Enchanted Palace

ISBN 978-0-545-53553-3

12 11 10 9 8 7 6 5 4 3 2 1   14 15 16 17 18 19/0

Printed in the U.S.A.   40
First Scholastic printing, February 2014

Enchanted Palace

ROSIE BANKS

Scholastic Inc.

Contents

A Mysterious Find

"I think I'm finished now, ma'am. Where would you like this box to go?" Summer Hammond asked as she packed up the last two books from her station.

"I'm finished here, too," Jasmine Smith added, putting the last things into a box.

Mrs. Benson smiled. "Goodness! That was fast work, girls. Well done."

Ellie Macdonald poked her head up from behind a table, tucking a wiry red curl behind her ear. "Hey, nobody told me it was a race!" Laughter danced in her green eyes as she stood up.

Jasmine winked at Summer. "It looks like we're the champions!"

"You're all champions," Mrs. Benson said as she smiled at the three girls. "This was the school's most successful rummage sale ever, and it was all thanks to you!"

Although they were all very different from one another, Ellie, Summer, and Jasmine were as close as sisters. They all lived in the same town and had been best friends since they first started elementary school.

Summer was shy, and tugged at her blond braids whenever she felt nervous. She often had her head buried in a book, either reading about the natural world or writing poems and stories about her animal friends.

Jasmine was outgoing and always in a hurry, with her long dark hair whipping around her as she raced from one thing to another. She loved singing and dancing and being in the spotlight.

Ellie was a joker, and was always the first to laugh at her own clumsiness. She was also very artistic and loved drawing. Together the girls made quite a team!

"It was nothing really," Summer said, blushing at their teacher's praise. "The books I sold were mostly my old ones from our attic."

"Well, they were very popular," said Mrs. Benson. "And, Jasmine, you played that guitar wonderfully. After everyone heard you, we sold it in no time."

Jasmine grinned. "No problem, Mrs. Benson. You know I love music!"

"And the fashion boutique was a great success, too — especially those superb Ellie Macdonald designs!" Mrs. Benson picked up a T-shirt with a bold green-and-purple pattern on it. She looked over at Ellie. "Thanks so much for making one for me."

"Do you like the design?" Ellie said. "Green and purple are my favorite colors."

"You don't say!" Jasmine's hazel eyes

twinkled with amusement as she looked at her friend's flowery purple-and-green dress, her green leggings, and her purple ballet flats!

Ellie chuckled, then turned to pick up her bag. But as she did, she tripped over something and fell to the floor with a *thump.*

"Ouch!"

"Are you okay?" asked Mrs. Benson.

"I'm fine — it's just my two left feet, as usual!" Ellie said as she stood up. "But what's this?"

She picked up the object she'd tripped over — an old wooden box. It was as large as her outstretched hand and made out of solid wood with a curved lid. The whole thing was thick with dust, but under the grime Ellie could tell the box was beautiful. Its sides were carved with intricate patterns that she couldn't quite make out, and on the lid was a mirror, surrounded by six glass stones. Ellie wiped the lid with her sleeve and could just see her reflection. As she held the box, light swirled in the stones. It looked almost . . . magical. "How strange," she murmured. "I'm sure it wasn't here a minute ago."

Jasmine took the box and tried to open it. "The lid's stuck down," she said. "It won't budge."

Mrs. Benson glanced at her watch. "Well, wherever it came from, it's too late to sell it now. Why don't you girls take it home — you never know, you might find a way to open it."

"Ooh, yes please!" Summer breathed. "It's really pretty. We could use it to put jewelry in. Let's take it to my house and try to get it open. I live the closest!"

The girls waved good-bye to Mrs. Benson and raced out of the school playground. They all lived in a small town called Honeyvale, which was surrounded by hills and beautiful countryside. Summer's house was only a few minutes away from the school, just past the post office and Mrs. Mill's sweet shop. Mrs. Mill waved as the girls flew by — she was used to seeing Summer, Ellie, and Jasmine together!

When they arrived at her house, Summer eagerly opened her front door and they pounded up the stairs, calling out a quick hello to Mrs. Hammond before spilling into Summer's bedroom.

The walls were covered in wildlife posters, and books were stacked neatly on their shelves. Summer dropped down onto her white fluffy rug. Jasmine and Ellie joined her, placing the carved wooden box in front of them. Summer's cat, Rosa, came over and sniffed at it with interest.

"What do we do now?" Ellie asked.

Jasmine grabbed a box of tissues from Summer's bedside table. "We clean it."

The three friends worked together, wiping away the dust and dirt that covered the box.

"Wow. It's absolutely gorgeous!" exclaimed Summer. She traced her finger over the side of the box. Now that it was clean, she could see that the sides were covered in delicate carvings of fairies, unicorns, and other magical creatures.

The glass stones that studded the lid were a deep green, and shone like emeralds.

"What do you think is inside?" Ellie whispered.

Jasmine shrugged. "Let's try opening it again."

Ellie passed Jasmine a ruler from Summer's desk and they carefully tried to pry the lid open, but it refused to budge.

Summer sighed. "There has to be a way to open it." She rubbed at the mirrored glass of the lid with a tissue to clean away the last traces of dust, then gasped. "The mirror. It's . . . glowing!"

"It is," squeaked Ellie, staring wide-eyed at the box. "And look — there are words in it!"

Jasmine frowned. With a shaky voice she read out the words that had appeared:

"Ten digits make two,
Though two are too few.
But three lots of two,
On each jewel will do."

The three friends looked at one another in amazement.

"Is–is it a trick?" Summer stammered.

"Or maybe magic?" Ellie whispered.

"I don't know," Jasmine said thoughtfully. "But the words look like a riddle. My grandmother is always giving me Hindi riddles to solve. She says it's good for my brain."

"Do you think you can solve this one?" Ellie asked.

Jasmine stared at the words. "Well," she began, "Grandma says that riddles don't always mean what they seem to mean. You've got to look at things sideways. 'Ten digits make two . . .' Well, the word *digits* normally means 'numbers,' but it can also mean 'fingers,' right?"

Summer and Ellie nodded.

Jasmine sat up a bit straighter. "So if 'ten digits' refers to your fingers and thumbs, that would make two . . ."

"Hands!" Ellie finished. "Ten digits make two hands! 'Though two are too few,' so two hands aren't enough!"

" 'But three lots of two, on each jewel will do,' " said Summer. "So 'three lots of two' means three sets of hands."

Ellie's eyes gleamed. "That's it! The riddle is telling the three of us to put our hands on the green jewels!"

"What are we waiting for?" Jasmine said. "Let's do it!" She placed her hands on two of the glinting stones. Ellie and Summer hesitated for a moment but then lowered their palms to the jewels, too.

Their hands completely covered the box.

It might just have been Jasmine's and Ellie's hands next to hers, but it seemed to Summer that the box was growing warmer underneath her touch. "Can you feel that?" she whispered. Ellie and Jasmine nodded, their eyes wide with amazement.

Suddenly, the mirror glowed brightly and light spilled out from between their fingers. Gasping, the girls moved their hands — and the box burst open! A beam of glittering light streamed out and bounced off the walls of Summer's bedroom. The girls watched in awe as the beam hit her wardrobe, and disappeared.

"Wow! Did you see that?" Ellie cried, staring down at the box, which was shut again as if nothing had happened. The others nodded. "I wonder if —"

Suddenly, she was interrupted by hangers clattering inside Summer's wardrobe.

"It's dark, so dark," wailed a deep voice.

"Please calm down, Your Majesty," a girl's tinkly voice replied. "I'll find a way out."

"Ouch!" cried the other voice. "Careful where you put your elbows, Trixibelle!"

Summer, Ellie, and Jasmine stared at one another in astonishment.

"Does your wardrobe normally do that?" Ellie asked Summer.

"Um, no. M-m-maybe we should hide?" Summer looked pale.

Just then, the wardrobe door wobbled, and all three girls leapt to their feet.

"Ah, here it is. I think I've found a way out," the tinkly voice said.

Jasmine narrowed her eyes. She grabbed Summer's ruler and held it out in front of her like a sword.

"Who's there?" she shouted bravely.

As if in answer, the wardrobe door sprang open and something small and colorful zoomed out into the air. Sparks flew everywhere as it whirled around the room. Then, silently and delicately, a tiny girl came to a stop above Summer's bedside table. A girl floating on a leaf!

Unexpected Visitors

The tiny person was hardly bigger than Summer's pencil case, but she was the most gorgeous creature that the girls had ever seen. Her messy blond hair peeked out from under a flower hat, which matched her colorful dress, pretty bracelets, and shiny ring. She had big, bright blue eyes, cute pointy ears, and a dazzling smile.

"She can't be real," Jasmine murmured, staring in wonder.

"Do you think she's a-a-a . . ." Summer could barely finish her sentence.

"A pixie?" The pretty creature smiled. "Yes! And of course I'm real," she said, doing a loop-the-loop on her leaf. "I'm Trixibelle — Trixi, for short — and I'm a royal pixie. And who are you?"

Ellie and Summer were too surprised to speak. There was an actual pixie in front of them! Finally, Jasmine, who was always the boldest, stepped forward and introduced herself.

"I'm Jasmine. And this is Ellie and Summer." She pointed at her friends.

"Summer, Jasmine, and Ellie," Trixi repeated. Suddenly the large, shiny ring on her finger twinkled with magic. She tapped it and a burst of sparkles shot out, forming their names in glittery writing in the air. "What lovely names!"

The three friends gasped in delight as the sparkles floated down and landed on their skin like snowflakes.

"Trixi! Where have you gone?" a voice yelped from inside the wardrobe. There was a *crash* and a pile of clothes tumbled out the door. A small, rosy-cheeked man, the same height as Jasmine, emerged from under the clothes. He was dressed in a purple velvet robe trimmed with white feathers, and he wore half-moon spectacles perched on the end of his nose. He had a pointy beard, and a gleaming crown sat at a jaunty angle on his thick, curly, white hair.

Trixi gave a little curtsy. "May I present King Merry, ruler of the Secret Kingdom," she said, zooming over to him on her leaf and pulling a yellow sock off one of the points of his crown.

The girls looked at one another, then quickly curtsied as well.

"Pleased to meet you," Jasmine said in her most polite voice. "But what are you doing in Summer's bedroom?"

"And what on earth is the Secret Kingdom?" Ellie added, finally finding her voice.

The king adjusted his spectacles and peered at the girls. But instead of answering their questions, he said, "Oh my. Are you humans? Trixi, what's going on?"

"I believe we are in the Other Realm, Sire," Trixi said, her face shining with excitement.

"Goodness me!" said King Merry. "No one from our kingdom has visited the Other Realm for a very long time." He stared at the girls. "You see, the Secret Kingdom and your world, which we call the Other Realm, exist side by side but our paths rarely cross. I don't know how we've come to be here."

Trixi looked around the room and spotted the carved box on the rug. "Look! There's your Magic Box, Your Majesty. Its power must have brought us here."

"This box belongs to you?" Summer asked, looking confused.

"Yes, it does," the king said with a pleased smile.

"And what sort of Magic Box is it?" said Jasmine, looking at it.

"It's one of my inventions!" King Merry said proudly. "I'm not exactly sure what it does yet, though." He sighed. "I invented it because I need something to show me a way to save my kingdom from Queen Malice's meanness. The next thing I knew, the box had disappeared, and we were in your wardrobe!"

"Wait a minute," Ellie said. "Who's Queen Malice?"

"She's my sister." King Merry took off his crown and anxiously rubbed at his forehead. "You see, my home is a place of great beauty. A place where unicorns graze in emerald fields and mermaids live in aquamarine seas. But my sister, Malice, can't bear to see that beauty. She wants to make everything as dull and dreary as she is, and take all happiness from the land." King Merry stopped, his eyes welling up.

Trixi quickly tapped her ring and a white hanky appeared. King Merry blew his nose noisily before continuing.

"Ever since the people of the Secret Kingdom chose me as their ruler instead of her, she has tried to get revenge on us all by using her magic to make everyone miserable."

Trixi folded her arms angrily. "And now, on King Merry's thousandth birthday, Queen Malice has done the worst thing ever! She's used her mean magic to make six horrible thunderbolts and fired them all into the kingdom. Each one carries a powerful spell designed to cause a terrible problem. But we don't know where they've landed or what trouble they will cause."

The king picked up the Magic Box and examined it closely. "I hoped this box could help me, but instead I've ended up in the Other Realm! It's baffling." He held the box out toward the girls. "You might as well keep it. It can't help me if its magic has gone all wonky."

Summer, Jasmine, and Ellie all leaned over to look at the box. Almost instantly a ripple of light spread across the box's lid, and another riddle appeared in the mirror! Ellie read it aloud:

"Look no further than your nose,
Look no further than your toes!
When you gaze at me you'll see,
The answer's clear as one, two, three!"

King Merry stamped his foot. "See! The box is all wonky! It's total nonsense!"

"It's a riddle, Your Majesty," Jasmine explained. "We've already solved one of them. I think we should try to solve this one — it could be a clue."

King Merry frowned. "All right. Well, since I invented the box, I suppose I should give it a try."

Jasmine nodded.

"Hmm . . . 'no further than your nose . . . no further than your toes . . .'" the king murmured.

The girls watched doubtfully as he crossed his eyes to look at his nose, then leaned forward to peer at his feet.

"Whoops!" The king's arms began to whirl like windmills as he tried to keep his balance. He fell onto the rug with a *bump.* "I told you it was nonsense," King Merry said sulkily, crossing his arms.

Jasmine, Summer, and Ellie looked down at the mysterious box again.

"'When you gaze at me you'll see, the answer's clear as one, two, three!'" Ellie said. "That's it!"

"What's it?" asked King Merry, looking confused.

"I think the Magic Box is saying that the three of us can help you!" Ellie cried, pointing at the mirror's reflection of herself and her friends.

"Of course!" Trixi clapped her hands in delight. "The king's inventions never normally work this well!" she whispered in Ellie's ear.

"What was that, Trixi?" asked King Merry, raising his eyebrows.

Trixi tried to look innocent. "Nothing, Sire. I was just saying that your inventions always work in the end."

The king considered Trixi's words and then smiled. "Yes, yes, indeed they do!"

Then he peered at the girls over his spectacles. "The Secret Kingdom is in terrible trouble. Queen Malice will stop at nothing to spread unhappiness. I rather think that you three girls may be our only hope! Will you help us?"

Ellie glanced eagerly at both of her friends. "We'll do anything we can!"

The Place You
Love Most

"You try and stop us!" Jasmine cried.

Even Summer was excited, despite still being a bit uncertain. "Can we go now?" she asked. "I can't wait to meet all the magical creatures, and —"

She stopped as the mirror on the Magic Box started flashing again, and another riddle appeared. Summer read it out loud:

"The thunderbolt is hidden close,
In the place the king loves most.
Magic made to stop the fun,
Must be found before day's done."

Trixi frowned. "Well, King Merry loves the Secret Kingdom more than anywhere else, but it's so big. We'll never find the thunderbolt."

"I think the riddle must mean somewhere special," Jasmine said slowly. "Where's your favorite place in the Secret Kingdom, King Merry?"

"Oh, that's easy," the king replied. "It's the Wandering Waterfalls." He scratched his head. "Um, hang on . . . I do love the Topaz Downs. And the Mystic Meadows are wonderful during a pixie toadstool fight." The king shook his head. "Oh dear,

I can't decide," he wailed. "There are so many places I love in the Secret Kingdom. I wish I was back in my palace, on my special snuggly throne. I always think best there."

"Maybe that's because you're happiest there," Ellie said, her eyes lighting up. "Perhaps your palace is the place you love most."

"Why, I think you're right!" the king exclaimed happily.

Trixi bit her lip anxiously. "But King Merry's birthday party is being held at the palace today! If the first thunderbolt is hidden there, Queen Malice's spell will ruin everything! We must leave for the Secret Kingdom right away."

Jasmine felt a buzz of excitement go through her. "How are we going to get there? Are we going to use magic?"

"Hang on, we can't just leave," Summer said, suddenly thinking of her mom and brothers, who were downstairs. "What do we tell our parents?"

"Don't worry," said Trixi. "My magic combined with the power of the Magic Box will easily transport you to the Secret Kingdom. And while the three of you are there, time will stand still in your world — nobody will even notice that you're gone."

Ellie's eyes sparkled. "Then what are we waiting for?"

She held out the Magic Box to Trixi, who tapped the lid with her ring and chanted:

"The evil queen has trouble planned.
Brave helpers fly to save our land!"

Trixi's words appeared on the mirrored lid and then soared toward the ceiling. Then the letters separated and descended like a cloud of sparkly butterflies. They began to whiz around the girls' heads until they formed a whirlwind.

"Place the Magic Box on the ground and hold one another's hands," Trixi called.

The whirlwind now filled the whole

room. Jasmine squeaked in delight as
she felt her feet leaving the ground. She
looked around and saw that Summer and
Ellie had also been picked up by the
magical storm. She squeezed their hands
encouragingly and her friends grinned

back. The king had his hands over his eyes, and Trixi was hovering just above his shoulder.

"Secret Kingdom, here we come!" Jasmine cried.

Then, in a flash of light, they were gone!

The Secret Kingdom

With a gentle bump, Jasmine landed on something soft, white, and feathery. "Wow!" she squealed. The girls were each sitting on the back of a giant swan, soaring through a bluebell-colored sky.

King Merry was riding another swan, which was bigger than the others and the tips of its wings sparkled with golden feathers.

"Enjoying the ride?" Trixi asked Summer, as she zipped along next to them on her leaf.

Summer nodded enthusiastically. "Where did these swans come from?" she asked, staring at their snowy whiteness.

"They're King Merry's royal swans," Trixi replied. "They're taking us to his palace."

"They're so beautiful," Summer murmured, reaching out and stroking her swan's downy back.

"This is AMAZING!" Jasmine shouted as her swan took the lead, soaring through the clouds. "It's so much better than the SkyRyde at the Honeyvale Fair!"

"I'm not sure about that," Ellie wailed, her face pale as she clung on tightly to her swan. "At least the SkyRyde ends after three minutes."

"You're doing really well, Ellie," Summer called over encouragingly, knowing that her friend was afraid of heights. "But you should look if you can — it's so beautiful!"

Ellie peeked over her swan's broad wing and gasped. Beneath them was a beautiful island, shaped like a crescent moon and set in an aquamarine sea. The shore of the island glittered with golden sand, and in the distance the girls could see emerald-green hills and fields filled with little balls of light on golden stems.

"They must be *sun* flowers," Ellie said to herself, giggling. For a moment, she even forgot how high up they were!

As they descended through the fluffy white clouds, Jasmine felt her stomach flip-flop as she saw mermaids — real mermaids — sitting on shimmering rocks, combing their silvery hair. She could even hear their voices singing a hauntingly beautiful song.

"Welcome to the Secret Kingdom," Trixi said with a grin.

As they swooped down over the island, a fluttering flock of dragonflies rose up to meet them. A medley of colors surrounded them and Summer giggled in delight as one delicately landed on her hair.

"It's the most gorgeous hair clip ever!" Ellie laughed as she admired the dragonfly's beautiful, colorful wings.

King Merry proudly pointed out areas of the kingdom as they passed: the fairy flying school at the Windy Weir; Magic Mountain, filled with sparkling snow-covered slopes and ice slides; and Unicorn Valley, with its racecourse and enormous magical tree.

"Wow! Is that your palace, King Merry?" Jasmine asked, pointing to a fairytale castle nestled between two hills. A deep sapphire-blue moat hugged the castle walls, and magic seemed to glitter on the coral-pink bricks of the palace. The golden spires of the four palace turrets were studded with rubies and shone in the bright sunlight.

King Merry nodded. "Home, sweet home."

The swans landed safely in front of the palace gates and Ellie slipped gratefully to the ground, followed by Summer and Jasmine.

Trixi flew over to them. "Did you enjoy that, girls?"

"The kingdom is beautiful," Ellie said. "But I'm very happy to be on the ground again!"

"You must be joking, Ellie," Jasmine exclaimed with a grin. "I thought it was the best thing ever. I can't wait to ride on a swan again!"

"And it's just the beginning!" King Merry boomed. "Follow me."

He led them over to the gates. The golden railings twisted upward into the shape of a mighty oak. As the king pushed them open, the branches flowered and a fanfare sounded all around them.

"The king is here!" Trixi announced as they walked into the beautiful courtyard.

A group of friendly, green elf butlers, dressed in long black coats and white gloves, all turned and bowed. Then they returned to hanging streamers in the trees.

As the three girls looked closely, they saw that hundreds of glowing fireflies were clinging to the strings to make little lights.

"Oh my," the king breathed. "How handsome the twinkle-twinkle bunting looks. Trixi, my suggestion for the streamers has worked beautifully!"

"I never doubted that your idea would work, Sire," Trixi said. She hovered above Ellie's shoulder. "It just needed a bit of pixie magic to help it along," she added in a whisper.

Ellie giggled.

As the king led everyone farther into the courtyard, they passed a huge fountain surrounded by a cloud of sweet-smelling bubbles.

"Hang on a minute," said Jasmine. "That's not water, is it?"

Trixi smiled. "No. It's lemonade!"

"A lemonade fountain!" Ellie cried, running back and forth, trying to catch one of the fragrant bubbles on her tongue. Summer and Jasmine laughed as they watched their friend.

Behind them came the *clip-clop* of hooves, and they turned to see a beautiful blue pony led by an elf butler, which was pulling a wagon loaded with brightly wrapped packages.

"My birthday presents!" King Merry exclaimed excitedly.

But Summer wasn't interested in the gifts. She couldn't take her eyes off the pony and its aquamarine mane.

"He's gorgeous." She smiled.

"And he looks really friendly," Ellie added, staring into the pony's warm brown eyes.

Smiling, Trixi tapped her pixie ring and a rosy-red apple appeared in each girl's palm. But just as they started feeding them to the pony, Jasmine felt a chill suddenly crawl up her neck. A dark shadow fell over the courtyard.

"Oh no!" cried King Merry. He pointed to the sky.

Floating over the palace was an enormous thundercloud. On top of the ugly gray cloud the girls could see a tall, thin woman with a spiky silver crown and a mess of frizzy black hair.

"Oh no," Trixi whispered. "Queen Malice is here!"

Party Games

Jasmine, Ellie, and Summer stared up at Queen Malice on her cloud, their hearts beating fast. Lightning crackled all around, giving the girls the shivers. Thunder rumbled loudly as the cloud stopped above King Merry's palace just long enough for a burst of rain to pour right onto his presents.

"Your birthday party is ruined, brother!"
Queen Malice shouted at King Merry.
"Just you wait and see!"

"What do you think she did?" Summer
asked the others. But neither Ellie nor
Jasmine could guess.

Queen Malice gave a cackle of
mocking laughter, then the gray cloud
sped off.

Suddenly the presents in the wagon
began to shake and rustle. There was
the sound of tearing as little legs pushed
through the wrapping paper. Then the
gifts leapt from the cart and ran away!

"My presents!" King Merry wailed.

Trixi tapped her ring. Although a
stream of purple glitter flowed from it,
nothing happened to the gifts. "My pixie

magic isn't strong enough to undo Queen Malice's spells!" she cried.

Without thinking, Ellie dived forward and caught one of the escaping gifts. As soon as she did, the legs disappeared and the present sat innocently in her hands.

"Quick," Jasmine said. "We've got to catch the rest!"

Everyone leapt after the fleeing gifts.
Jasmine and Summer managed to herd
three into a corner and pick them up.
One ran straight through the legs of a
surprised-looking elf butler. Ellie, who
was following it, couldn't stop in time and
knocked him over! King Merry caught
one by jumping on it, and then looked
sadly at the present, which was now
squashed flat.

"At least I can fix that," Trixi told
him, tapping her ring and repairing it
magically.

Eventually all the presents were caught
and changed back to normal. The girls
stacked them back on the wagon.

Trixi blew her hair out of her eyes. "I
wish we could find a way to stop Queen
Malice once and for all," she said fiercely.

"And her horrible helpers, the Storm Sprites. The queen has all kinds of mean tricks up her sleeve, and we never know where she'll turn up next."

"She is such a bully," said King Merry. "And she's determined to ruin my birthday. I just know that cursed thunderbolt of hers is hidden here somewhere, all ready to cause trouble." The king's eyes brimmed with tears. "This is going to be the worst party ever — my subjects are going to be miserable, and they won't have any fun."

"Yes, they will," Ellie said, her eyes flashing. "Because we're going to find the thunderbolt and stop it from doing any harm!"

"That's right," Summer and Jasmine chorused in loud, firm voices.

"And I'll help, too," Trixi said, floating up to the king's face and drying his tears away.

"Thank you, girls," said King Merry, but his voice was still shaky.

"Bobbins!" Trixi called to one of the elf butlers.

The elf rushed over and bowed deeply.

"King Merry needs a cup of hot cocoa with extra marshmallows," Trixi explained. "And then he needs to change into his party clothes. His guests will be arriving in two hours!"

Bobbins led the king away into the palace.

"Let's go and find that thunderbolt!" Trixi said as she dusted off her hands. "We should start in the palace gardens, since that's where the guests will gather later. Remember to keep an eye out for trouble!"

She stood up on her leaf and sped ahead, leading the girls out of the courtyard and into a maze with twisting and turning paths that seemed to change every time they blinked. Summer, Ellie, and Jasmine looked down every path and under all the hedges, but there was no sign of the thunderbolt anywhere.

Trixi led them out of the maze and past a beautiful pond that had a rainbow leading down into its depths. Trixi explained that the rainbow was a magical slide that could take you anywhere in the Secret Kingdom you wanted to go.

Finally, the girls walked into a garden filled with trees made of cotton candy.

Bunting hung from the trees, and a group of brownies were busy putting lots of cakes onto a long table.

"These ones look amazing," Ellie said, pointing to a cluster of pink-frosted cupcakes.

"They're cupcakes," Trixi explained.

"Oh, we have those at home," Jasmine said, sounding a bit disappointed.

"Really?" Trixi said. "The magical kind? If you eat one, you'll be able to fly for five minutes!"

"Wow!" Jasmine exclaimed. "We definitely don't have cupcakes like that! Can we try them?"

Trixi nodded. "Just one bite, though, we don't want the magic lasting too long. We've got a thunderbolt to find!"

Jasmine grinned excitedly and offered

the cupcakes to her friends, but Ellie shook her head. "Flying like a fairy? No thanks, I'm happy to have my feet on the ground!"

Jasmine took a small bite of her cupcake. After a moment's hesitation, Summer did the same. Instantly, a pair of glittering wings sprang out on each of their backs.

Jasmine flapped her wings carefully, and then shot upward. Summer was soon beside her and they zoomed through the air, going higher and higher. The wind whipped through their hair as they did loop-the-loops and whooped with excitement.

Trixi twirled in the air with them, and then came to land on Ellie's shoulder. "Don't go too high up," she called to Jasmine and Summer.

Just as Trixi spoke, Summer began to wobble. "Uh-oh, my wings are shrinking!" she cried out.

"Jasmine, look out!" Ellie shouted as her friend's wings disappeared.

"Don't worry, Ellie," Trixi said. She tapped her ring and Jasmine and Summer suddenly slowed and landed gently on the ground.

"Whew!" Jasmine said, then grinned. "That was so much fun!"

Trixi winked at the girls. "Flying with leaves is much safer." She giggled.

Summer chuckled, although her legs still felt wobbly. "I think you're right!"

At the other end of the table, Ellie pointed to some heart-shaped treats. "Hey, what are these called?"

"Endless cookies," a brownie piped up. He only came up to Ellie's knee. He was covered in soft brown hair and wore a funny green cap. "You can eat as many as you want and never get full. Would you like one?"

"Yes, please!" Ellie took one and popped it into her mouth. "Yum! It tastes like strawberries and chocolate and ice cream all rolled into one!"

Trixi and the girls continued to look around the palace grounds, searching for any sign of Queen Malice's thunderbolt or the problems it might be causing, but there was still no trace of it. Eventually they reached an orchard where party games were being set up.

They could see a large barrel where seven dwarfs were practicing bobbing for golden apples. Nearby, two tiny pixie girls were busy wrapping one of their friends in glittery pink paper.

"What are they doing?" Summer asked.

"They're getting ready to play Pass the Pixie, of course!" Trixi said. "It's a great honor to be chosen as the pixie in the package."

Ellie grinned as she spotted a cheeky-looking imp drawing a unicorn on a wall. When the picture was complete, the unicorn stamped its hooves and nodded its regal head.

"Let me guess." She smiled. "Pin the Tail on the Unicorn?"

Trixi nodded. "We'll also have Musical Thrones and Blind Brownie's Bluff. Then, of course, there's Musical Statues, but I've made the gnomes promise to change the guests back to normal right after the game is finished this time." Trixi shook her head. "It's really no fun being a statue for too long — I hate staying still!"

Ellie and Jasmine laughed, but Summer's forehead creased with worry. "What are we going to do? The party starts soon, and we still haven't found the thunderbolt."

"We just have to keep looking," Trixi said. "We know it has to be somewhere around the palace. Malice's nasty magic will reveal itself soon enough."

Suddenly, a loud burst of laughter whipped through the air.

"What was that?" Ellie asked urgently. "Is it Queen Malice?"

Trixi crinkled her little brow. "No, it didn't sound like her."

The wild laugh sounded again.

"It's coming from over there," Summer said, pointing to an iron gate with ivy curling over the top.

"That's the Outdoor Theater, where the king's royal performers are putting on a show to begin the birthday celebrations," Trixi said, flying toward the arched entrance. "Come on, we need to find out what's happening!"

Ellie, Summer, and Jasmine raced toward the archway and then stopped in horror. There, sticking in the ground next to the entrance, was a jagged black thunderbolt!

Malice's Nasty Surprise

As Ellie, Summer, and Jasmine stared at Queen Malice's horrible thunderbolt, another loud laugh came from the theater.

"We have to find out what trouble the thunderbolt's caused," Ellie exclaimed.

"At least someone sounds happy. . . ." Summer said hopefully.

They stepped through the gates. Rows of marble seats led down to a wide stage. All around them, performers lay in heaps, tears streaming from their eyes.

"We've got the — hee-hee — the g-g-giggles," a leprechaun managed to squeak between screeches of laughter. "A-a-and we don't know why!" The little man held his aching sides. "The sh-show — hee-hee-hee — starts in half an hour, and all of our scenery has been covered with black paint."

Trixi looked angry. "Queen Malice," she hissed. "She's trying to ruin the show." She tapped her ring and chanted a spell:

"With this magic, hear my plea,
Stop laughing and act normally!"

A shower of purple glitter spread through the air and settled on the performers. But they still couldn't stop laughing.

"Malice's magic is much too powerful for me. We're going to have to cancel the performance." Trixi shook her head in despair. "It was supposed to be the grand opening to the party. King Merry's palace is usually full of laughter — and Queen Malice has turned that into a bad thing. King Merry will be heartbroken."

"Wait," Jasmine said. "We can't let Queen Malice win. Maybe magic isn't the only way to stop her."

"What do you mean, Jasmine?" Summer asked.

"The four of us can put on the show ourselves," Jasmine announced.

Ellie nodded, a smile stretching across her face. "If you can get me some paint and brushes," she said, "I can easily paint some new scenery."

"And I can write you a song to perform, Jasmine," Summer offered.

Jasmine glanced over at the giggling performers. "I think we'll need a dance as well. I can make something up."

Trixi's face bloomed with happiness. "And I'll help you all in any way I can! First, paint and brushes!" Trixi tapped her ring and instantly several brushes and pots of bright colors appeared.

Ellie knelt down and gathered them up. "Perfect!" She hurried over to the stage, stepping over a giggling elf. There were six backdrops at the rear of the stage. Ellie shook her head in disgust as she saw that they had all been covered with big splashes of black paint.

Ellie squeezed her eyes shut and tried to remember all the wonderful places she'd seen from the back of her swan. In no time at all she had painted a whole new scene showing the mermaids she had seen in the beautiful greenish-blue sea.

"One down, five to go," Ellie said to herself determinedly.

Meanwhile, Jasmine had started practicing some tricky dance moves. Her face was serious as she concentrated on making the steps as polished as possible.

Summer chewed on a pencil as she tried to think of lyrics for a new song. She looked up at the sky, hoping that the words might jump into her head. Her eyes widened. Even though it was daytime and the sun was shining, she could also see shooting stars and the moon glowing brightly in the sky. She blinked as she saw a face appear in the white surface of the moon and wink down at her. Summer

smiled and eagerly scribbled something
down. She knew exactly what the song's
chorus would be!

Trixi whizzed between the girls, helping
out where she could. Finally, the scenery,
dance, and song were all finished.

"We've sorted out the show, but what
about the poor performers?" kindhearted
Summer asked. She nodded at the actors,
stagehands, and musicians, who were still
lying on the ground giggling.

"At least they're happy!" Trixi smiled
as an elf gave a squeal of laughter. "But
we need to get them backstage — and
quickly! The king's guests will be here
soon." She tapped her ring and conjured
up some floating stretchers, which carried
off the giggling performers. Trixi and the
girls quickly followed them.

From the wings of the stage, they watched as the guests took their seats. The audience let out a huge cheer as King Merry arrived, wearing his ceremonial robes, which were so long they almost tripped him as he walked!

Trixi floated behind him, holding up the end of his robes like a wedding dress as he made his way to his seat, looking very excited.

Trixi tapped her ring and two spotlights burst to life. "It's showtime!" she said.

Jasmine took a deep breath and marched out onto the stage. She felt braver when she saw Ellie's beautiful backdrops, with their paintings of mermaids, glittering golden beaches, and snowcapped mountains.

From the wings, Summer and Ellie peered into the crowd. They had never seen an audience like it. To the right, there were two real–life unicorns. To the left, a group of fairies with bright shimmering wings whispered excitedly. In the front row were the youngest pixies, elves, dwarfs, and imps.

On the stage, Jasmine didn't have long to take it all in. She had to start the show.

"Thank you for coming here from all over the Secret Kingdom," Jasmine called out. "Welcome to the start of King Merry's birthday party!" She threw her arms wide, just as she'd seen performers do on TV. The audience cheered in approval. Whispers rippled through the crowd.

Trixi grinned at Summer and Ellie. "The crowd loves her! I don't think they've ever seen a human girl before."

"We have quite a show for you tonight," Jasmine continued. "But first I must tell you about something that almost stopped it from going ahead at all."

King Merry's face went pale, but Jasmine caught his eye and winked reassuringly. She swiftly explained how

Queen Malice's magic had given the royal performers a bad case of the giggles and damaged the scenery.

"My friends Summer, Ellie, Trixi, and I have put together a new show for you!" Jasmine said with a flourish. "We're not going to let Queen Malice ruin the king's birthday, are we?"

"NOOOOO!" the crowd roared.

"That's the spirit!" Jasmine said, beaming at the crowd. "We have a very special song for the king. But before I start, I think I need some backup singers. Summer and Ellie, will you come out and join me?"

Summer felt her cheeks go warm. She reached up quickly to twirl one of her braids. "I can't perform in front of all those people," she whispered.

"Yes, you can," Ellie urged. "Come on!" She dragged Summer onto the stage, and Trixi conjured up microphones for them both.

Jasmine grinned at her friends. "Trixi? Hit it!"

Trixi tapped her ring, and all at once the instruments floated up from the sides of the stage and began to play a cheerful melody. With one more burst of glitter from Trixi's ring, another sparkly microphone appeared in the air, and Jasmine caught it.

The three girls began to sing Summer's song. It was all about the Secret Kingdom and the places the king loved best. The audience thought it was wonderful and soon started singing along with the chorus:

*"The Secret Kingdom
is a magical place,
Even the moon has a smiley face.
The king's birthday will
be a day of fun,
Malice's meanness will be undone."*

While the instruments kept playing,
Jasmine handed her microphone to Ellie
and began her
dance routine.
Her dark
hair
whipped
all around
her as she
skipped
across the
stage.

The crowd clapped wildly in approval.

Ellie gave Summer a big grin. "We've done it. We've stopped Queen Malice from ruining the party and —"

SPLAT!

Ellie was interrupted by something hitting the scenery.

She and Summer looked up. Six strange-looking creatures with spiky hair, batlike wings, and ugly faces had swooped down into the open-air theater, riding on mini thunderclouds. Their eyes were shining with mischief and their mouths were twisted into angry scowls.

Jasmine hadn't noticed them yet because she was far too

busy dancing. But Summer could see that in their hands they held big fat raindrops, which they began hurling toward the stage!

"Trixi!" Summer hissed, beckoning to the pixie, who was hovering nearby. "Who are they?"

"Oh no!" Trixi's face fell. "Those are Storm Sprites, Queen Malice's servants." The pixie looked worried. "And if we get hit by one of their misery drops, we'll be made as sad and mean as she is."

"We've got to stop them!" Ellie cried.

Summer nodded and looked over at Jasmine. A misery drop was whizzing straight toward her!

Ducking and Diving

"Jasmine!" shouted Summer. "Duck!"

Jasmine heard the warning just in time and dove to the ground as the misery drop sailed over her head, missing her by inches. Immediately she jumped back to her feet and tap-danced on the spot, trying to keep the show going.

"Those are Queen Malice's Storm Sprites!" Ellie called to her, pointing up at the sky toward where the creatures were hovering.

Trixi flew over to Jasmine. "We have to get off the stage. Getting hit by one of those misery drops would be really bad news."

Jasmine kept on tap-dancing. "We can't stop," she said. "We can't let them ruin everything!"

From the stage, Ellie and Summer saw King Merry fall out of his chair as he dodged one of the Storm Sprites' misery drops.

Drops were now splashing into the audience, causing little rain clouds to spring up over everyone's heads. Soon unicorns, pixies, and elves were all looking miserable.

Up on the stage, Jasmine began to dance faster. "Hey, sprites!" she called. "Bet you can't get me!"

The six Storm Sprites narrowed their eyes and flew toward her.

"We're going to soak you!" one of the sprites said with a sneer. "Splish, splash, splosh!" He hurled a misery drop at Jasmine, but she jumped out of the way.

"Careful!" another sprite screeched. "You almost got me." The two sprites began to argue.

"That's it!" Jasmine said to herself. "If we can get the sprites to throw the drops at one another, we can turn their magic back on them!"

"Jasmine, come on!" Summer called as she and Ellie dodged and dived to avoid the misery drops splattered around them. "Duck!"

But Jasmine stood absolutely still.

"Jasmine, what are you doing?" Ellie called.

"Quick, get beside me and wait for my shout," Jasmine said. To her left she could see three Storm Sprites whizzing toward her on their rain clouds, misery drops raised. Another three were coming at her from the right. Ellie and Summer raced over to stand next to her.

"They're going to splash us!" Ellie cried.

"One . . . two . . . three . . . DUCK!" Jasmine shouted.

All three girls dropped to the ground just as all the sprites released their misery drops. There was a great *SPLAT,* and then a series of loud wails. All six sprites had been hit, and each one was soaking wet! Little storm clouds broke out over each sprite's head.

"Ugh!" one sprite whined. "I'm all cold and wet! I've got water up my nose. Look, I can blow bubbles."

"Me too," said the sprite next to him, letting all his drops fall to the ground and sitting on his cloud gloomily.

Jasmine rushed forward, scooped up his misery drops, and passed some to Summer and Ellie.

"Take that!" she yelled as they pelted the Storm Sprites with misery drops.

"Argh!" yelled a sprite. "This is horrible. Let's get out of here!"

The sprites' rain clouds rose into the air and zoomed quickly out of sight.

"Yes!" Jasmine cheered. "We did it!"

Ellie jumped up and down in delight.

But Summer was staring at the misery drop in her hands with a twinkle in her eye. "I have an idea," she whispered. "Maybe the misery drops can cure the performers' giggles."

"Let's ask Trixi," Jasmine suggested, waving her over.

The little pixie was helping King Merry, who had been hit with a misery drop and was sitting unhappily in a puddle with a cloud raining down on his head.

"He's so sad!" Trixi sighed as she flew over to the girls.

Summer quickly explained her plan and Trixi's eyes shone brightly. "Good idea, Summer!"

Summer held out the shining droplet,

and Trixi pointed at it. Her pixie ring gleamed as she chanted:

"Go to the performers, misery drop,
And make their silly laughing stop!"

The drop vanished, and there was a loud cracking sound from outside the theater.

"What was that noise?" Summer asked, pulling her two friends to their feet.

"I think I know," said Trixi. She darted to the theater gates, and reappeared with a mass of ugly black splinters floating behind her in a cloud of dust. "They're from Queen Malice's thunderbolt," she explained.

"Yuck!" Summer said, peering at the splinters. "Even now, it still looks nasty. But what happened to it?"

"When you girls helped the performers and stopped Queen Malice from ruining the show, it broke her spell," explained Trixi. "And the thunderbolt must have shattered."

Trixi tapped her ring and the splinters disappeared in a puff of smoke.

An angry shriek sounded, and suddenly a storm cloud appeared overhead with a familiar figure on top. It was Queen Malice, shaking her bony fist. "You human girls may have broken my first thunderbolt," she screeched, "but next time you won't be so lucky. My next one is hidden so well that you'll never find it!" She threw her head back and laughed as she zoomed away on her cloud.

Trixi shuddered.

"Don't worry, Trixi," Jasmine said fiercely. "We won't let her ruin the Secret Kingdom."

The others nodded.

"Oh, look." Summer smiled. "The performers — they've all stopped laughing."

Everyone turned to watch the royal performers walking out onto the stage. They were all shaking their heads as if waking up from a bad dream.

In the audience, the rain clouds had disappeared from above King Merry and the rest of the audience, and they all looked happy once again.

"Now that the thunderbolt is broken, all of Queen Malice's mean magic is undone!" Trixi said happily.

"Great," Jasmine said with a grin. "Now that everyone's back to normal, we can do a grand finale to the show!" She turned to the audience. "Sorry about the interruption, everybody. I think we should all sing along for this one. Are you ready?"

The crowd cheered. Jasmine whispered something to Trixi, and the little pixie tapped her ring. The instruments immediately struck up a familiar tune, and the whole audience sang "Happy Birthday" to King Merry. His face broke into a smile and tears of joy rolled down his plump cheeks.

After the show had finished, King Merry

came backstage to congratulate Summer, Jasmine, and Ellie.

"If it weren't for them, Sire, we would never have destroyed Queen Malice's thunderbolt," Trixi said.

The King smiled. "The Magic Box was very wise indeed when it took us to the girls. Summer, Jasmine, and Ellie, will you continue to be friends to the Secret Kingdom, and help stop my sister from causing more trouble?"

"Definitely," said Jasmine.

"I can't wait to come back!" Ellie grinned.

"We'll be here anytime you need us," added Summer.

The king nodded. "But you must promise to keep the Secret Kingdom a secret."

"We promise," Jasmine vowed. King Merry nodded at Trixi, and she grinned and tapped her pixie ring.

Suddenly, out of nowhere, three beautiful tiaras appeared in the air above the girls! Each one was surrounded by a sparkling glow. Summer's was a delicate rosy-gold color, with beautiful pink, heart-shaped jewels. Ellie's had fancy swirls and a green, diamond-shaped jewel in the center. Jasmine's was a shimmering gold with intricate loops and pretty opals that seemed to sparkle with all the colors of the rainbow.

The girls gasped as the tiaras settled carefully on top of their heads. They fitted perfectly!

King Merry smiled. "These tiaras will appear whenever you are here, and they will show everyone that you are VIFs of the Secret Kingdom, on important royal business."

"VIFs?" Jasmine wondered out loud.

"Very Important Friends," Trixi whispered.

"Wow!" said Ellie, taking her tiara off to look at it. "This is the most beautiful thing I've ever seen!"

Jasmine and Summer smiled broadly as they looked at each other's tiaras. "Thank you so much, King Merry!"

Trixi smiled at the girls and did a little somersault of delight. "I'm so pleased that you will visit us again," she said. "I'll be here to guide you every step of the way. And this will help as well."

Trixi pointed her ring toward the beautiful pictures of the Secret Kingdom that Ellie had painted as backdrops for the show. As the girls watched, the pictures flew up into the air in a burst of twinkles. And as they floated down, the pictures joined together and grew smaller and smaller, then landed in Summer's hands.

"It's a map of the Secret Kingdom!" Summer exclaimed.

But as the girls looked at the map closely, they realized that it wasn't an ordinary map — it was moving! The sea around the island had blue waves that lapped against the shore. The trees of the forests swayed in a breeze, and the meadows of sunflowers gleamed.

"There are five more of Queen Malice's nasty thunderbolts somewhere in the kingdom, just waiting to cause trouble," Trixi continued. "The Magic Box will tell you when it has located one, and the map will help you find out where it is."

The girls nodded. "We'll be back whenever we're needed," Summer promised.

"Good-bye, girls," Trixi said, flying up to kiss each of them on the tip of her nose. "See you very soon!"

With a tap of her ring, Trixi conjured up a whirlwind that scooped the girls up into the air, higher and higher. Then, with a bright flash of light, they found themselves landing gently back in Summer's bedroom.

Jasmine stared down at the Magic Box, which was still sitting on the fluffy white rug, exactly where they had left it.

"Did all that just happen, or was I having a strange dream?" she said. She put her hand up to feel for her tiara, but it was gone.

"It really happened," Summer breathed. "Look!" She held up the map of the kingdom.

"Where should we keep it?" Ellie asked. "It'll have to be somewhere secret. You heard what King Merry said — nobody can know about the Secret Kingdom except us."

As she spoke, the mirror on the Magic Box glowed. Then, to the girls' amazement, the box slowly opened, revealing six little wooden compartments,

all of different sizes! A shower of light
sparkled from the center of the box.

"It's the perfect place to store our gift!"
Summer exclaimed.

Ellie gently placed the folded map into
one of the spaces. It fitted perfectly! As
soon as the map was in place, the lid on
the box closed again.

"I wonder when the Magic Box will tell

us that it's time for our next adventure," said Jasmine.

"I hope it's soon," Summer said, crossing her fingers.

Ellie looked at the mirrored lid of the Magic Box and for a moment thought she saw King Merry's kind face beaming out at her.

"The Secret Kingdom needs us," she said softly. "I have a feeling we'll be back there very soon."

In the next Secret Kingdom
adventure, Ellie, Summer, and
Jasmine visit

Unicorn Valley

Read on for a sneak peek. . . .

A New Adventure!

"There!" said Ellie Macdonald, standing
back to admire the pretty shapes laid out
on the baking tray.

It was a rainy Sunday afternoon and
her best friends, Summer Hammond
and Jasmine Smith, had come over to
bake cookies. Summer had designed hers
in the shape of hearts, while Jasmine had

made crowns. Artistic Ellie had created cookie fairies with pretty wings.

"How long do we bake them for?" asked Summer, twirling one of her blond braids thoughtfully. "I don't want them to burn!"

"Fifteen minutes," said Ellie, consulting the cookbook.

"Fifteen minutes!" wailed Jasmine dramatically, slumping down in her chair so that her glossy black hair flew around her face. "But I'm *starving*!"

"It'll go by in a flash." Ellie giggled. "I'll get the timer."

She jumped up from the table where they had been working, then stumbled as she caught her foot on the leg of her chair.

"Oops," she said as it clattered to the

floor. Mrs. Macdonald came in to see what the noise was. "Don't you worry, girls," she said, admiring the cookies. "I'll put these in to bake, and call you when they're done. I'm sure they'll be delicious, and you've made such lovely shapes! Crowns and hearts and even fairies. What imaginations you all have."

While Mrs. Macdonald was putting the cookies into the oven, the three friends exchanged a grin. Of course Ellie's mom thought they had good imaginations — she hadn't been to the Secret Kingdom, the magical land where only a few days ago the girls had actually met a real king wearing a real crown, seen fairies, and eaten magical heart-shaped endless cookies at King Merry's birthday party!

"Let's go upstairs while the cookies are baking," suggested Jasmine loudly. "And check on the Magic Box," she added quietly as the girls headed up to Ellie's room. "Just in case! You did bring it, didn't you, Summer?"

"Of course," Summer said with a smile.

Ellie's bedroom was long and light, with her art books and tools scattered across a big desk and the colorful pictures she'd painted pinned all over the lilac walls.

The girls settled down on the big window seat where Ellie did her painting. Summer carefully pulled the Magic Box out of her bag and passed it to Jasmine, who stared eagerly at its mirrored lid.

The box was just as beautiful as when they had first found it. Its wooden sides were delicately carved with images of magical creatures, and its curved lid had a mirror surrounded by six glittering green stones.

"It was so lucky we found this at the school rummage sale." Summer smiled.

"We didn't find it — it found us!" Jasmine reminded her. "The Magic Box knew we were the only ones who could help the Secret Kingdom."

Read

Unicorn Valley

to find out what
happens next!

Be in on the secret.
Collect them all!

Enjoy six sparkling adventures.

Character Profile:
Ellie Macdonald

Family:
Ellie lives with her parents and little sister, Molly.

Favorite Colors:
Green and purple

Loves:
Painting and drawing

Favorite Place in the Secret Kingdom:
Mermaid Reef

Personality:
Quirky and creative. When everyone else is baffled by a problem, Ellie is often the one to find a brilliant solution.

Character Quiz

Jasmine, Ellie, and Summer are all heroes! But which one are you most like? Take our quiz to find out.

A baby bird has fallen out of its nest! Do you . . . ?

A — Take it home and look after it. You can't bear to see an animal in pain.
B — Climb back up the tree and put it in its nest.
C — Run for help — you really want to get the bird back to its nest, but you're not going up there!

Everyone's performing in a talent show! What would your talent be?

A — You couldn't possibly perform in front of people — you'll help backstage.
B — Singing and dancing — you want to be the star of the show!
C — Painting.

What's your favorite color?

A — Sunshine yellow.
B — Hot pink.
C — Purple and green.

What's your favorite hobby?

A — Visiting the pet store to see all the cuddly animals.
B — Going to dance class.
C — Designing your own clothes.

Which personality traits best describe you?

A — Shy and quiet.
B — Outgoing and energetic.
C — Funny and clever.

Mostly As

You are Summer!
You are kind and thoughtful,
and you love animals!
You're sometimes a little
bit quieter than your friends,
but you still love hanging
out with them and
having fun in the
Secret Kingdom.

Mostly Bs

You are Jasmine! You are
brave and energetic. You
love being the center of
attention, especially when it
comes to singing
and dancing.

Mostly Cs

You are Ellie! You are funny
and clever, and you're
artistic, too! Even though
you're scared of heights,
you're brave enough to do
things that scare you.

RAINBOW magic™

Which Magical Fairies Have You Met?

- ❏ The Rainbow Fairies
- ❏ The Weather Fairies
- ❏ The Jewel Fairies
- ❏ The Pet Fairies
- ❏ The Dance Fairies
- ❏ The Music Fairies
- ❏ The Sports Fairies
- ❏ The Party Fairies
- ❏ The Ocean Fairies
- ❏ The Night Fairies
- ❏ The Magical Animal Fairies
- ❏ The Princess Fairies
- ❏ The Superstar Fairies
- ❏ The Fashion Fairies
- ❏ The Sugar & Spice Fairies

📖 SCHOLASTIC

Find all of your favorite fairy friends at
scholastic.com/rainbowmagic

RMFAIRY9

RAINBOW magic™

SPECIAL EDITION

Which Magical Fairies Have You Met?

3 stories in each one!

- ☐ Joy the Summer Vacation Fairy
- ☐ Holly the Christmas Fairy
- ☐ Kylie the Carnival Fairy
- ☐ Stella the Star Fairy
- ☐ Shannon the Ocean Fairy
- ☐ Trixie the Halloween Fairy
- ☐ Gabriella the Snow Kingdom Fairy
- ☐ Juliet the Valentine Fairy
- ☐ Mia the Bridesmaid Fairy
- ☐ Flora the Dress-Up Fairy
- ☐ Paige the Christmas Play Fairy
- ☐ Emma the Easter Fairy
- ☐ Cara the Camp Fairy
- ☐ Destiny the Rock Star Fairy
- ☐ Belle the Birthday Fairy
- ☐ Olympia the Games Fairy
- ☐ Selena the Sleepover Fairy
- ☐ Cheryl the Christmas Tree Fairy
- ☐ Florence the Friendship Fairy
- ☐ Lindsay the Luck Fairy
- ☐ Brianna the Tooth Fairy
- ☐ Autumn the Falling Leaves Fairy
- ☐ Keira the Movie Star Fairy
- ☐ Addison the April Fool's Day Fairy

 SCHOLASTIC

Find all of your favorite fairy friends at
scholastic.com/rainbowmagic

 HiT entertainment

RMSPECIAL12

The Rescue Princesses

These are no ordinary princesses—
they're Rescue Princesses!